Bloomsbury Publishing, London, New Delhi, New York and Sydney

First published in Great Britain in September 2012 by Bloomsbury Publishing Plc
50 Bedford Square, London, WC1B 3DP

Text & illustrations copyright © Debi Gliori 2012

The moral right of the author/illustrator has been asserted

A CIP catalogue record for this book is available from the British Library

ISBN 978 1 4088 1940 1

Printed in China by Hung Hing Printing (China) Co Ltd, Shenzhen, Guangdong

1 3 5 7 9 10 8 6 4 2

FSC
MIX
Paper from
responsible sources
www.fsc.org   FSC® C101807

www.bloomsbury.com
www.debiglioribooks.com

For Frank S. Barker –
the original party animal –
with lots of love

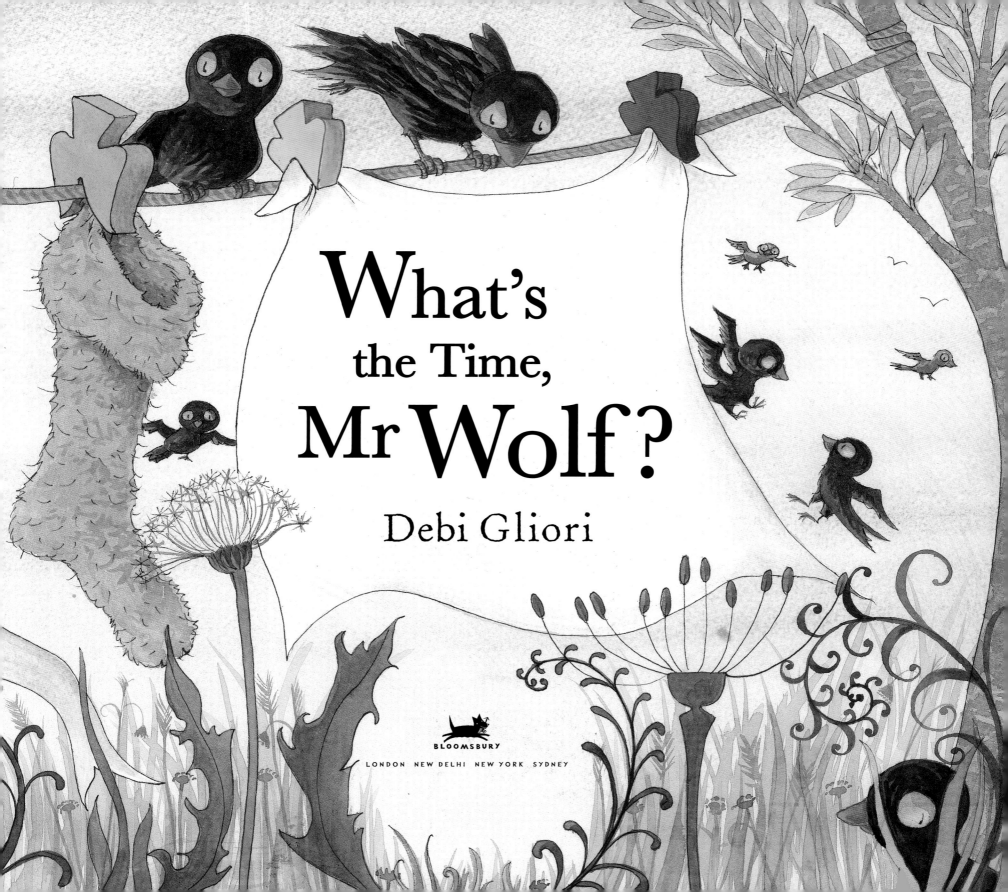

What's the Time, Mr Wolf?

Debi Gliori

BLOOMSBURY

LONDON NEW DELHI NEW YORK SYDNEY

It is **seven** o'clock in the morning.
Mr Wolf is woken up by four and twenty blackbirds.

'What's the time, Mr Wolf?' they tweet.
'It's time for blackbird pie,' yawns Mr Wolf.

It is **eight** o'clock in the morning.
All Mr Wolf's neighbours slam
their doors on their way to work.

BANG!

goes the door
of the stone house.

CRASH!

goes the door of the
wooden house.

THUD!

goes the door of the straw house.

'What's the time, Mr Wolf?'
giggle the three little pigs.
'It's time for bacon sandwiches,'
mutters Mr Wolf.

It is **nine** o'clock in the morning.

Here comes the post girl in her little red hood.

About time too,
thinks Mr Wolf,
running to the door.

But there is nothing for Mr Wolf —
not so much as a card!
Poor Mr Wolf.

It is **ten** o'clock in the morning.
Mr Wolf is trimming the hairs on his
chinny-chin-chin when his phone rings.

Mr Wolf hears a **snort**, then an **oink** and a **giggle**.

Finally a voice squeals,
'What's the TIME, Mr Wolf?'
'Not you lot again,' groans Mr Wolf.
'It's time you little pigs bought a watch. Goodbye.'
And he puts the phone down.

It is **eleven** o'clock in the morning.

Mr Wolf's tummy gives a loud rumble.
What's the time, Mr Wolf? he wonders.
Time for a snack?

But when he goes to
his cupboard, it is bare –
even his dish has run off
with his spoon!

It is **twelve** o'clock.
Midday.
Time to go shopping,
thinks Mr Wolf.

He is halfway to the shops
when it starts to rain.
Time I bought an umbrella,
thinks Mr Wolf.

It is
one o'clock
in the afternoon.

BONGGGG!

There's a mouse
running up
Mr Wolf's clock.

'What's the time,
Mr Wolf?' squeaks
the mouse.
But Mr Wolf
doesn't answer.
Mr Wolf is out.

It is **two** o'clock in the afternoon.
Mr Wolf is in the cake shop.

'What's the hurry, Mr Wolf?' says the baker man.

'I'm baking your cake as fast as I can,
patting and prodding and filling with jam,
bake for an hour then remove from the pan.'

It is **three** o'clock
in the afternoon.

Mr Wolf is tired and very, very hungry.
He is heading home when …
ZOOOOOOM! WHOOOOOOSH!
A crowd rushes past.

'No time to stop, Mr Wolf,' they gasp. 'We're already late.'

It is **four** o'clock in the afternoon.
Mr Wolf takes the shortcut home.
It is cool and shady under the trees.

'Time for a nap,' says Mr Wolf.
He is nearly asleep when...

HEY DIDDLE-EE
DIDDLE-EE DIDDLE-EE
YOWWWL!

Mr Wolf's eyes spring open.
There is a cat playing the fiddle.
'**Five** o'clock. Time to wake up,
Mr Wolf,' the cat says.
'Shall I play some more lovely
tunes on my fiddle?'

Mr Wolf shudders.
'Good grief!' he says.
'Is that the time?
Awfully sorry. Must dash.'
And he runs away
as fast as he can.

It is **six** o'clock.

BONG, goes Mr Wolf's clock.

BONGGG! BONGGG!

BONGGG! BONGGG!

TWONgggk!

'SSHHHhhhhh!'

say Mr Wolf's friends.

Mr Wolf is nearly home. He climbs the step, lifts the latch, opens his door and ...

'WHAT'S THE TIME, MR WOLF?'

It's PARTY time!

And later. Much later.
All Mr Wolf's friends have gone home.

Mr Wolf is brushing his teeth.

Mr Wolf is pulling up the quilt.

'What's the time, Mr Wolf?'
say the stars.
But Mr Wolf doesn't reply
because Mr Wolf is fast asleep.

It is BEDtime.